Juarez

Written by

Bill Stinson

Illustrated by

CHICK

DEDICATED TO

Beau

Ryan

Remy

Harper

Lila

Logan

Brett

The words echoed throughout the large horse stable.

Crestwood Racing Stables

Startled, a small burro arose from his straw bed near the front of the stable. He picked up a bright pail of oats marked "UNO" and slowly made his way to the middle stall.

Shouts were soon
heard from all of the stalls.
"Donkey, bring me my oats!"
The small burro picked up a
pail of oats for every horse
and carried one to each stall.

Juarez was a small burro who lived in the stable with many valuable horses. Every day, he would deliver and pick up the oat pails for all of the horses.

After delivering the pails, Juarez usually rested under a large oak tree in the front of the stable yard until the horses finished eating their oats. His return trip was never enjoyable.

"Donkey, my pail is empty," shouted Uno as he kicked the empty pail toward Juarez. "You didn't bring enough oats this morning."

"My name is Juarez, and I'm a burro," he said to Uno as he picked up the empty oat pail.

"My name is Juarez, and I'm a burro," mocked Uno. He kicked hay from his stall toward Juarez.

The other horses in the stable laughed loudly and began to make fun of the small burro.

Juarez picked up all of the empty pails and carried them to his stall.

He emptied any remaining oats from the pails into a corner of his stall.

"Juarez, you rascal!" shouted Julio as he pushed open the stable door. "Come here! I need a big, strong burro to help pull my tractor out of a ditch."

Juarez trotted to where Julio was waiting. He liked it when Julio rubbed him on the head between his ears.

Julio was the foreman of Crestwood Racing Stables, a prestigious thoroughbred racing stable that competed in horse races around the world. He cared for and trained a stable of fifty-six horses.

Uno was the fastest horse in the world.

"I will need to put a rope around your strong shoulders, so you can pull my tractor as I try to drive it out of the ditch," said Julio. He hugged Juarez.

Julio climbed into the seat of the tractor, which sat tilted in the ditch. Juarez jumped when Julio started the engine.

"Pull, Juarez!" Julio shouted over the loud noise of the tractor engine.

Julio waved for Juarez to move forward.
Juarez pulled as hard as he could, but the tractor failed to move.

Juarez closed his big brown eyes, planted his legs in the soft ground, and pulled with all of his strength.

Julio screamed, "Pull, Juarez! Pull!"

The tension on the rope relaxed, and Julio was able to drive the tractor out of the ditch.

"I knew you could do it!" screamed Julio as he jumped from the tractor and ran toward Juarez. "You are one strong burro."

"I have a special treat for you."
Julio pulled two orange carrots
from his pocket.

"Eat these while
I remove the ropes from your
strong neck and shoulders."

Julio tossed the ropes on the tractor. "Sorry, but you will have to walk back to the stable."

"Thanks for the oats,"
squeaked Ty,
a brown mouse in the
corner of Juarez's stall.

"Yeah, thanks a lot," said a gray mouse named Mobe as she turned her head to watch Juarez enter the stall. "Uno is a mean horse. Do you want me to bite him tonight while he is sleeping?"

"No," said Juarez. "Uno is very important to Julio. He must take very good care of him." "Just a thought," said the gray mouse.

Juarez was tired. He lay down in his straw bed and dreamed he was a magnificent racing burro. The fastest burro in the—

"Donkey, bring me my oats!"
Uno screamed from his stall.
"I'm hungry, and you're late again."

Juarez stretched, then began to deliver the morning oat pails to the horses. When he returned from delivering the morning oat pails, he noticed that Julio had closed the front stable door.

Juarez could smell the rain.
He returned to his small stall and waited for the
horses to finish their morning meal. The wind
began to blow stronger, causing dirt and dust
in the stable to swirl.

He heard the rain as it began to hit on
the roof of the stable.
Thunder became loud in the distance.
Lightning now lit up the darkening sky.

Juarez got up and walked
through the stable.
Thunder and lightning made
the horses very nervous.

"Donkey," said Uno as Juarez walked in front of his stall, "I don't like storms."Juarez stopped and sniffed the air. Something was wrong! "Help me, donkey!" screamed a horse from the far end of the stable. "The stable is on fire."

Juarez saw a small fire at the end of the stable where the horse was tied. The flames were growing quickly, and the rest of the stable was beginning to fill with smoke.

"Help me! I can't get loose from my rope!" The horse screamed and kicked as it repeatedly jerked the rope holding it to the stable wall. Other horses were now beginning to scream for Juarez to help them.

"I'm coming!" yelled Juarez as he ran through the thickening smoke into the stall where the horse was tied.

"Stop jumping!" shouted Juarez as he began wrapping the rope around his neck and shoulders. Juarez tugged and the rope broke free from the wall.

"This way," he yelled above the increasing crackle of the fire. Juarez and the horse ran to the front of the stable. "Oh, no!" shouted Juarez. The front stable door was closed. Juarez turned and kicked at the stable door. Two kicks and the door flew open.

The horse passed Juarez and ran through the open doorway.

Juarez could feel the increasing heat from the flames. He quickly returned to the burning stable and snapped the ropes of the other horses.

Now only one horse remained.

"Hurry, donkey!" screamed Uno. "I can see the fire. I can feel the heat. I can smell the smoke. Hurry!"

Juarez looked up at Uno as he began to wrap the rope around his thick neck. "My name is Juarez, and I'm a burro."

Juarez gave a strong tug, and the rope came loose from the stable wall.

Uno jumped from his stall and ran faster than he had ever run toward the front stable door. As he passed through the stable doors, the stable began to collapse.

"Where is the donkey?" he asked as he turned to look at the collapsing stable. All of the horses had escaped, but the little burro was missing.

Juarez watched the stable burn as he stood in the pasture. He wasn't able to reach the front door, but he'd escaped through a small opening that had been burned near the back of the stable.

Julio and the other stable workers moved the horses to a different stable. Julio was sad. All of the horses were safe, but he was missing a small burro.

"There he is!" Havay pointed when he saw Juarez standing in the tall grass of the pasture the next morning. Julio climbed the wooden pasture fence and sprinted across the tall grass.

Julio wrapped his arms around Juarez's neck.
"I was worried that you didn't make it out of the fire."

"You're injured," Julio said as he inspected the dried bloody marks on the small burro's neck and shoulders. "Let's get you back to a stable and get these wounds covered."

"Wait... these aren't burns from the fire. These look like rope burns. You helped the horses escape. I noticed that their ropes were broken or were pulled from the wall. Only one strong burro could have done that. You saved all of the horses."

Months passed, and a new stable was built where the old stable had burned. Juarez had a new large stall in the front of the stable.

A pail marked "JUAREZ" hung from a nail on the front of his stall.

"Juarez...when you have finished eating your oats, would you please bring me my oats?" Asked Uno in a voice just above a whisper.

"I can wait."

"I still think I should have bitten him," said the fat gray mouse as she stuck her head out of a pile of oats.

Juarez smiled. He picked up the pail of oats marked "UNO" and trotted down the center of the stable.

UNO

All in a day's work!

THE DRAGON FROM NOWHERE

by Bill Stinson

Darcy and Keller visit Pap's
house for a few weeks during
the summer.
What they find living under the
lighthouse at Cape Nowhere,
South Carolina
will be the adventure of a
lifetime.

THE
DRAGON
FROM
NOWHERE

BY BILL STINSON
ILLUSTRATED BY RICH THOMPSON

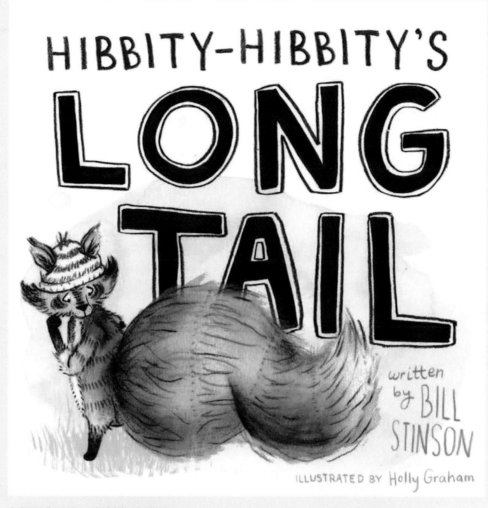

HIBBITY-HIBBITY'S LONG TAIL

written by BILL STINSON

ILLUSTRATED BY Holly Graham

Hibbity-Hibbity, by Bill Stinson **has a problem.**
All of the Hibbity-Hibbitys where he lives have short tails.
Something has hold of his short tail and will not turn loose.
Hibbity-Hibbity visits the forest where he discusses the
problems with his friends.
Join the fun as each of Hibbity-Hibbity's friends have a
hilarious solution to Hibbity-Hibbity's problem.

Deward

A young African boy is swept into the Atlantic Ocean by the raging Nabi River.

Clinging precariously to a sinking tree, he is rescued by a passing ship and taken to London.
Set in the 1600's, Deward eventually ends up in the New Colony of Georgia. This is the extraordinary story of a young boys growth to manhood and the choices he has to make.

Bill Stinson

Deward

Bill Stinson